A LITTLE STORY ABOUT

a BIG TURNIP

Retold by TATIANA ZUNSHINE
Illustrated by EVGENY ANTONENKOV

To my son **Phillip** – **T.Z.**

To my family – **Marina, Pavel,** and **Nikita** – **E.A.**

**Special thanks to Carlo Scaccia, Lusia Moskvicheva
and Will Zink for their invaluable help.**

First Edition

A Little Story About a Big Turnip / Tatiana Zunshine / Evgeny Antonenkov
Summary: Traditional Russian folktale presented in a non-traditional way

ISBN 0-9646010-0-1
Library of Congress Catalog Card Number: 95-92202

10 9 8 7 6 5 4 3 2 1

Book Design: Evgeny Antonenkov
Book Production: Peri Poloni

Pumpkin House, Ltd
P.O. Box 21373
Columbus, OH 43221-0373

Printed in Hong Kong.

There once lived a grandfather. Everybody called him **Grandie**.

He had a wife **Grannie**, and a granddaughter **Annie**,

and a dog **Ruffie**, and a cat **Meowsie**, and a mouse **Squeakie**.

They all lived in **a small house** with a backyard where they grew vegetables.

Once **Grandie** planted a turnip seed in his backyard.

The turnip grew

and grew

and became very,

very large.

One day **Grandie** decided to pull the turnip out.

He pulled, and pulled, and pulled... but the turnip wouldn't come out.

So **Grandie called** his wife **Grannie** to come and **help** him.

There came **Grannie** and they started pulling *together.*

Grandie pulled at the turnip,

Grannie pulled at Grandie, they pulled, and pulled, and pulled... but the turnip wouldn't come out.

So Grannie **called** their granddaughter **Annie** to come and **help** them.

There came **Annie** and they started *pulling together*.

Grandie pulled at the turnip, Grannie pulled at Grandie,

Annie pulled at Grannie,

they pulled, and pulled, and pulled...

but the turnip wouldn't come out.

So Annie **called** the dog **Ruffie** to come **and help them**.

There came Ruffie and they started pulling together.

Grandie pulled at the turnip,

Grannie pulled at Grandie,

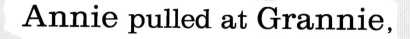

Annie pulled at Grannie,

Ruffie pulled at Annie,

they pulled,
 and pulled,
 and pulled...

**but the turnip
wouldn't come out.**

So Ruffie called the cat **Meowsie** to come and help them.

There came Meowsie and they started pulling together.

Grandie pulled at the turnip, Grannie pulled at Grandie,

Annie pulled at Grannie,

Ruffie pulled at Annie,

Meowsie pulled at Ruffie,

they pulled,

and pulled, and pulled...

**but the turnip
wouldn't come out.**

So **Meowsie** **called** the mouse **Squeakie** to come and help them.

There came Squeakie and they started pulling together.

Grandie pulled at the turnip, Grannie pulled at Grandie,

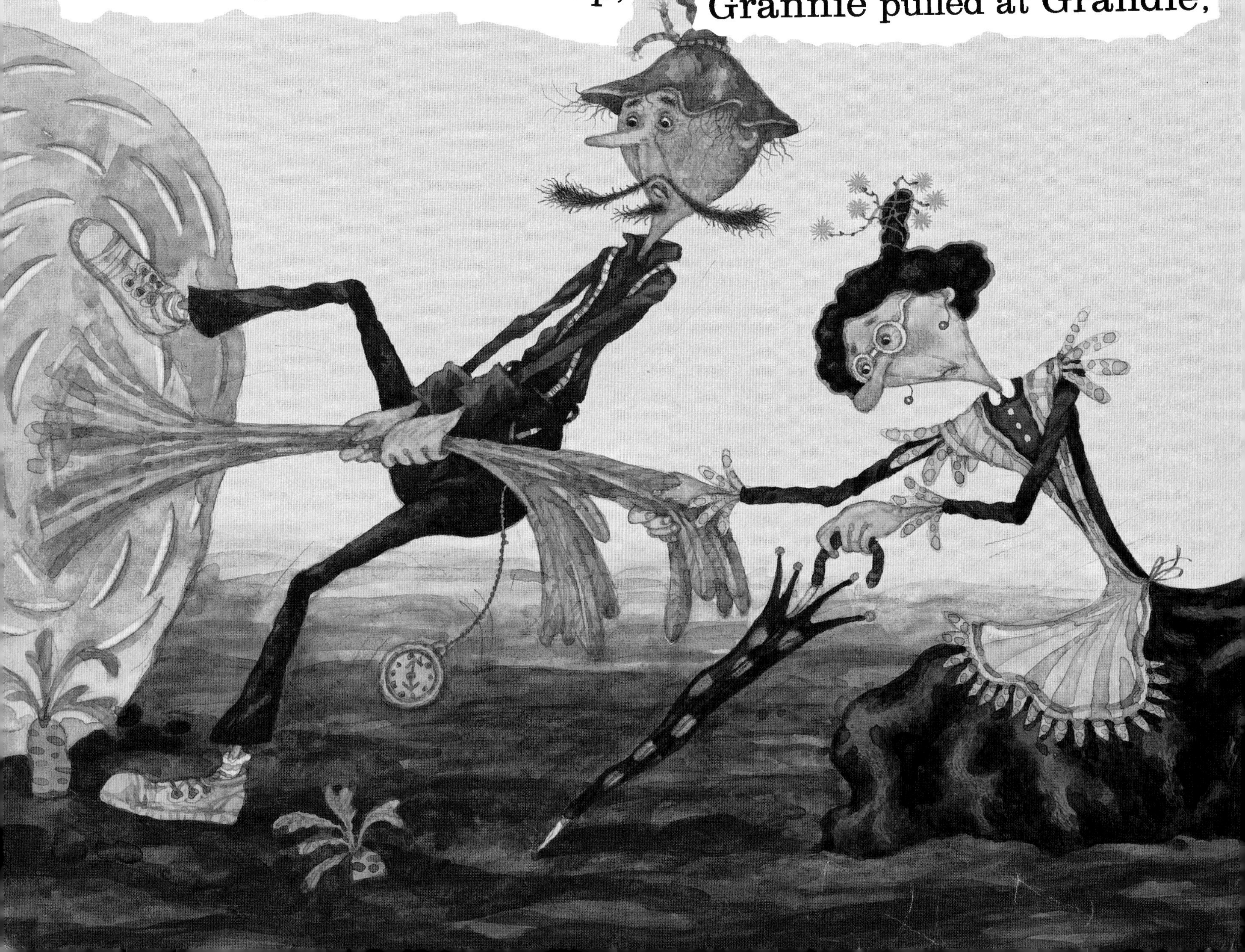

Annie pulled at Grannie,

Ruffie pulled at Annie,

Meowsie pulled at Ruffie,

Squeakie pulled at Meowsie,

they pulled,

and pulled, **and pulled**...

and the turnip

DID come out!!!

THE eND